Mr. Blacky
and
His Palace

written and illustrated by

L. J. West

Mr. Blacky and His Palace
is written and illustrated by L.J. West
Copyright 2006 L.J. West

Published and Printed by:
Lifevest Publishing
4901 E. Dry Creek Rd., #170
Centennial, CO 80122
www.lifevestpublishing.com

Printed in the United States of America

I.S.B.N. 1-59879-267-9

To Amanda, Rachel, and Griffin

One day when I was visiting
with Grandma, she asked me
if I would like to walk down
to the corn crib
to see Mr. Blacky.

I had been to the corn crib
with Grandma several times before,
but she had never mentioned
any Mr. Blacky to me.

We went to the corn crib all the time
but never to visit with Mr. Blacky.

We went almost every day
to get corn for the chickens.

Who could Mr. Blacky be?

Mr. Blacky sounded like a dog to me.

I bet Grandma has gotten herself another dog.

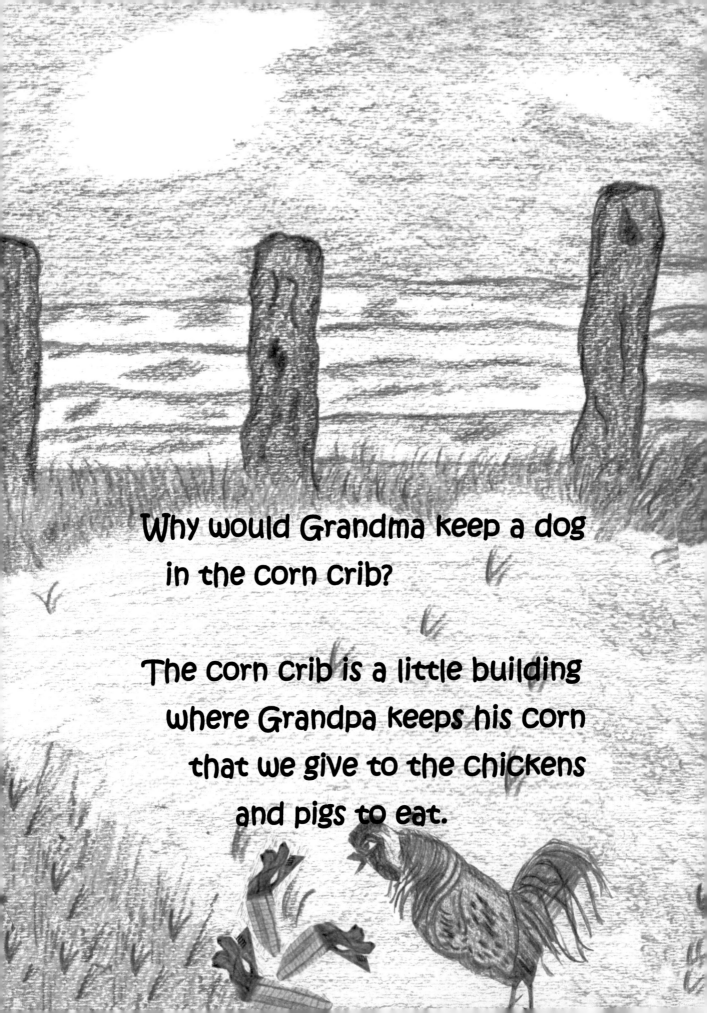

Why would Grandma keep a dog in the corn crib?

The corn crib is a little building where Grandpa keeps his corn that we give to the chickens and pigs to eat.

Grandma said,
   "Oh, you will like Mr. Blacky;
   he is so shiny and pretty."

Grandma also said that Mr. Blacky
   had a bed in the corn crib.

Again, I asked myself,
   "How could a dog have a bed
   in the corn crib?"

I didn't believe sleeping on top
of all those hard ears of corn
could be very comfortable
for any dog--big or small.

Grandpa had a lot of corn in the crib,
and there was no place
to have a bed,
except on top of the corn.

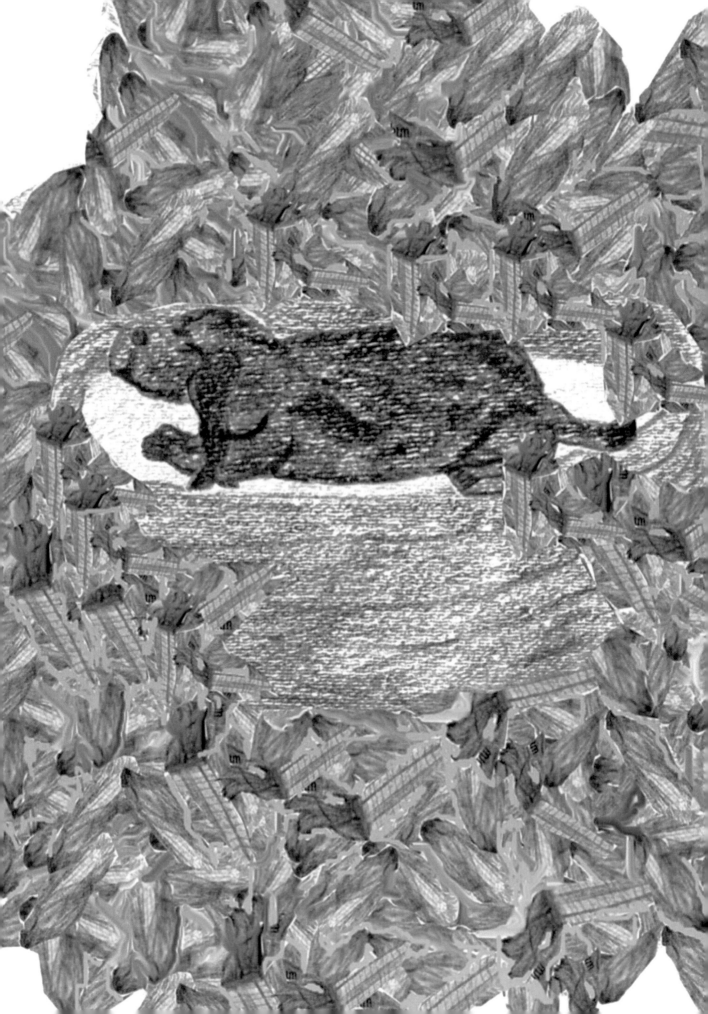

Grandma and I looked through
the opening that Grandpa
used to throw the corn
into the crib.

I anxiously looked around, but
I did not see a dog any place.

I asked Grandma,
"Where is Mr. Blacky?"

"I bet Mr. Blacky has gotten
loose and run away."

Grandma said, "Oh no,
   he has not run away. I see him."

"Look up very high."

"Look at the very top of the building."

I looked up, and to my surprise,
   there was not any dog
      but a big long snake!

He was all stretched out
   on the top rafter.

Mr. Blacky looked as if he were a king
   who was guarding his palace.

Mr. Blacky was a snake!
   A really, really big snake!

I was so excited!

I don't like snakes, but on that day I
found out that Grandma did.

I said to Grandma, "I see Grandpa
over at the barn. Let's go get him
  so he can get rid of that snake."

"Oh no," she said. "I want Mr. Blacky
  to stay around. He is one
   of the good snakes."

"Mr. Blacky stays up high,
so he can see the mice
as they come sneaking in
to get some corn to eat."

"All Mr. Blacky needs to do
is raise his head, and
the mice will run
fast as they can back outside
through their little holes."

Grandma continued to say,
"Why, if we didn't have Mr. Blacky,
I guess we would have nothing
but a bunch of big fat mice
running in and out of here
eating our corn."

Mr. Blacky crawled back up
to his favorite rafter to take
a nap after he had chased
the mice outside.

I was tired, too. Grandma decided
that we needed to sit down and
"rest" for awhile
just like Mr. Blacky.

Grandma wanted to know
if I would like to go back
to the corn crib with her
in the morning.

I guess I will go back
   to the corn crib with Grandma.

But before I get any corn out
   for the chickens or pigs,
   I am going to make sure
       to take a good look around
           to see where Mr. Blacky
               might be making his bed
               for the day.

I still don't like snakes!

Mr. Blacky
and
His Palace

by **L.J. West**

I.S.B.N. 1-59879-267-9

Order Online at:
www.authorstobelievein.com

By Phone Toll Free at:
1-877-843-1007